# Ruined Prom

## Taboo Older Man Fixes It

By LL Honi

# Contents

I didn't know it, but she'd been mine for most of her life. Things changed so quickly and what I wanted to do to her now was so very wrong. But I dutifully played my role and hoped my fantasies would be enough for me.  Then her boyfriend dumped her for the school bike.

I found her sobbing in her room; her tears broke me, they renewed me, they gave me purpose. I knew it was time to step up, time to take charge and do what only the man of the house could do. Make everything right.

I knew the way I was feeling was wrong, taboo but June wasn't related to me, well – only by marriage, but seeing her tears was enough.

Tonight I would make her night special. I would be her first, I would take her and make her mine forever.

# Chapter 1

It was my step-daughter June's prom night, how does the time fly?  It seemed like just yesterday that I'd married her mother Martha and gained a cherubic, 5-year-old, baby girl.  Now she was 18 and graduating high school.  June was always sunshine, smiles, sugar and spice – the best kind of little girl to have.  I doted on her and loved having her around me.

It became obvious that she worshipped me as well.  She followed me around *helping* me with all the chores and my hobbies at home.  She went on fishing, hiking and camping trips, never far from me.  As she grew older and her interests changed, she'd still find ways to be near me, reading her books or studying somewhere close by.

The closer June and I grew the more distance grew between Martha and I.  It wasn't that Martha was jealous, the age gap of 7 years just became insurmountable.  We had such different interests that there was nothing keeping our awareness of each other.

I got home early one weekend soon after June had turned 15.  Parking in the driveway I found Martha busy loading her luggage into her car.  She turned to me, bitterness clearly showing on her face. "We're done Jim, there's no point pretending any longer.  I'm leaving."

"But Martha… What do you mean 'you're leaving'? Where will you go? Can we at least talk about this?"

"**No**! Jim.  I'm sick of this, I'm leaving and you can't stop me.  Don't try and contact me either."

"But… Martha…" I stammered in shock, only now noticing that her small car was completely full.  With no room for a passenger. "Is June already gone?"

"June is almost fully grown so she can stay with you, she's more your daughter now than mine anyway with how the two of you dote on each other.  So you can just suck it up and take care of her full time.  Besides… I've fallen in love with a co-worker who'll put me first and we don't need a kid around messing with that. I put the divorce papers on the kitchen table, you just need to sign them."

I silently watched, stunned, as Martha got in her overfull car and drove away.  I turned and raced into the house, suddenly scared that she'd lied, calling Junes name.  When I saw her race out of the bathroom barely wrapped in a towel, clearly leaving her shower half finished, I was overcome with relief.

"What is it, Daddy?  What's happening?  Are you ok?"

"Oh, baby girl," I said gathering her close. "I'm so sorry, so I'm just going to say this straight.  Your mother's left us."

Her face crumpled as she broke, her legs collapsing under her.  I caught her as she fell and swept her up, cradling her tight before settling on the couch.  Cuddling her close in my arms, I struggled with my own sorrow as I tried to sooth her.

"I know it's a shock Junilette, but don't worry.  I'm here and you'll stay here. I'll take good care of you.  Ssshh, I love you.  You're *my* girl.  It'll be ok sweetling." I murmured, rubbing her back soothingly.

I looked down to gage how she was coping.  To my shock, the towel had gaping open across her front.  I could clearly see all of her; from her already large breasts, with their suckable raspberry drop nibbles, all the way down to her neatly contoured and shaved pussy. My mind blanked as my cock turn rock hard.

Oh! My! God!

I sat there with a raging erection and worked damn hard not to press it into her as I soothed and calmed her.  Trying so hard to pretend that I hadn't just seen the most perfect body I had ever laid eyes on. Straining so hard not to acknowledge visions and fantasies of fucking this wonderful girl and breeding my children on her.  It was so wrong to want to claim her as mine forever, even though I've loved her for so long.

June started stirring as her tears slowed to a stop and wrapped her arms around me, the movement pushes her succulent breasts fully against my chest. "It's ok Daddy, your only 39.  You always take care of me. I love you, you've always been my Daddy and I'll always be your girl."

Feeling her young body pressing against me left me flushed with guilty fantasies of the forbidden.  "That's right sweet girl.  We'll stay here and I'll take care of you."

"That's what Daddies do, but we'll take care of each other." At that she got up and went back to finish her shower, leaving me with damp clothes and a raging erection.

Quickly, I duck into the nearest room with a door, which turns out to be the laundry room.  I stare into space as I try and wrap my head around this new and excitingly taboo way of seeing my baby girl.  Lost in thought I unconsciously start rubbing my throbbing cock through my damp jeans.  I see June's panties lying in the laundry basket and grab them, guiltily I bring them to my face and inhale her sweet young scent.  My mind blanks and I tear my jeans open to release my thick, heavy cock. I fist that lacy scrap around my throbbing cock and start fucking my hand as I sub-come to a fantasy.

*"Oh June, look what you do to me.  Look at how hard I am for you.  I want you.  Push your tits together for me, I'm going to fuck them.  You want to be a good girl for Daddy, don't you?"*

*As she pushes her round globes together I lean forward and slide my 9 inch cock between them.*

*"June baby, suck my cock as I fuck your chest. That's right baby girl, suck my cock as I fuck you."*

*She's leaning against the washer for support as I hunch over her, shafting myself in her shower slicked tunnel.  Feeling her mouth surround my knob each time I surge forward.  I fumble one hand down to flick and pinch a nipple, but find her fingers already there, pinching and pulling on her nipples.*

*"Daddy... oh that feels so good.  Oh god... oh Daddy, I'm so wet... you taste so good.  I need you to fuck me, Daddy, I want your cum inside me.  I want to feel you flooding my body with your seed, feel it dripping from me, running down my legs as I overflow with your cum.  I want you to breed me, Daddy.  I want you to fill me so full of your cum that it can't help but take root."*

*I grab her, push her against the washer. Bending her young body over, as I use a knee to separate her arousal slick thighs and see her open cunt and pulsing clit waiting for my seed to fill her.  I lick her from clit to ass with the flat of my tongue before going back and pushing my tongue as deep as possible in her hot, tight hole, drinking her arousal down.*

*"Oh baby girl, I'll give you anything you want, you know that.  Look how wet and ready you are for me. I'm going to fuck you so hard that'll you'll never want to look at anyone else.  You're MY girl and I'll NEVER be tired of fucking you."*

*I slam my cock in her dripping hole in one sure thrust, bottoming out in her channel as my balls slam against her clit.  She screams and shudders in pleasure, mewling and writhing as I hold still.  I can feel her cervix against the head of my shaft.  I slowly pull out, savouring how she clutches and tightens around me as if trying to stop me from leaving the only home my 9 inches will ever have again.*

*"Oh Junie, you feel so good, made just for me.  I never want to take my cock from here.  I'm going to fuck you and fill you with my cum till it's pouring from you. Till it takes root inside you, breeding you.  Oh, June! I'm going to take you in so many ways that you'll never need another man ever."*

*I thrust hard into her, ploughing her young, tender pussy, showing her how a man fucks the woman he loves.  In turn, June writhes beneath me, egging me on with filthy, dirty language until I cum hard and long, flooding her fertile womb with my seed.*

I return to reality as I climax, jetting my seed across the laundry room in long white slashes.  I cum so hard that my legs weaken and it's me that's leaning against the washer for support.  I use June's panties to clean up and realise that things are going to get tough.

## Chapter 2

Freed from Martha's conservative tastes June started wearing flirtier clothes, designed to accentuate her blossoming assets.  As proud as I am of her blossoming confidence, her increasingly stylish and form fitting clothing choices cause havoc on my poor cock.  It spends more time erect than it did when I was a teen.

Months pass and we settle into a comfortable routine but it's everything I can do to suppress my desires, constantly struggling with the guilt of wanting what I shouldn't want. My dreams and fantasies of June's blossoming body, taking and breeding my beautiful girl take a toll on my sleep.  I take to spending a lot of time at the gym working out my frustrations and arousal by working my body.

It doesn't really work, the harder and more in shape that I get, the higher my testosterone gets and the more I'm becoming obsessed with her.  Wanting her, needing to feel her tight heat surrounding me as I fill her unused cunt and flooding her with my seed. Breeding my stepchild with a child of my own.  I know these desires are forbidden and wrong, but I can't stop thinking them.

June herself doesn't help in my bid to keep my hands off her.  She starts practicing her flirting with me, glancing touches, skimpy clothes, tiny sleepwear.  As she gets older and more developed, she starts making a concerted effort to temp me and her ploys against my resolve get stronger and clearer.

Walking into the kitchen, one morning months away from her 18th birthday, I see June bending over the dishwasher in a cami that barely covers her braless C cups, nipples hard and tenting her top.  The matching scrap of lace hugging her ass clearly outlining her full pussy lips.  Making it obvious that she's recently shaved, clearing it completely.  I almost break and drop to my knees and sink my face into her untouched cunt.  I love a clean pussy.  Nothing in the way as I feast, nothing to stop her juices from spreading and dripping from her aroused and leaking slit.

But my resolve is strong.  I stand firm.

Then, a week later and only months away from the end of school, she hits me with her biggest shock.

She's got a boyfriend.  She's given up on me.

I'm heartbroken.  All the changes she's been making to herself have caught the attention of some pubescent cocksucker too filled with testosterone and attitude to know what a princess he's got.  I'm beyond jealous, I want to keep her all to myself but I force myself to do what's right and support her in her new relationship.  The only positive is that she eases off on torturing me.

It soon became clear to me that the boyfriend, Bruce, doesn't know how to treat June.  June, on the other hand, was smitten.  Thrilled to finally have a boyfriend, she accepted his coarse behaviour, leering looks and rough language.  I hoped like hell that this would run its course, after all June was a smart girl who was raised to know her worth. Knowing anything I said against him would drive her further into his arms but it took great strength of will to keep my silence.

On her 18th birthday, her friends got together and threw a special birthday party down by the river.  I knew I would have to turn a fairly blind eye to what happens if I don't want to spoil her special night by being an over protective father.  The only saving grace was good cell reception and knowing that my sweet girl was very responsible and not inclined to misbehave.

She's been hiding in her room for hours, preparing for her party.  She didn't tell me what she'd chosen to wear tonight, keeping it a surprise for me.  I have to admit, that did make me fairly nervous.  Bruce finally rocks up, late, and she finally comes out of her bedroom.  I'm floored.

She's so beautiful.  She's wearing a mid-length sundress that perfectly complements her dark colouring, tight in all the right places, showcasing her feminine body in a clean and flattering way.  She's stunning, sexy and classy all in one.  I just hope that Bruce doesn't fuck up her night.

"Have fun baby girl and remember, call me if you need anything.  No matter the time"

***

It's close to 2 am when I get a distressed and tearful phone call from June begging me to pick her up.  Bruce had vanished from the party leaving her alone, surrounded by drunk idiots, and without a ride home.  Knowing neither an Uber nor a Cab will go out to the river at this time of night, I quickly throw on a shirt and shorts and go.  When I arrive it's even worse than it sounded, the fires have died down and everyone has either passed out or left.  My princess is standing all alone in the near dark.  She clings to me tear stained and trembling.  I keep a calm front and take her home.

I snuggle her against me the whole way home, gently telling her how every thing's fine.  That she's safe, just generally being a great and understanding dad. When we get home we sit on the couch hugging as she finishes calming down.

"Thank you, Daddy, I knew you'd come get me.  Although I do hope Bruce is ok, there must have been some kind of emergency for him to leave me like that."

I knew she was wrong, but what could I do?  Turns out he told her straight out he'd been bored and went to score some weed.  And, angel that she is, she forgives him.  I just can't wrap my head around it.  He should be worshipping the ground she walks on, forever grateful that a special girl like her would even grace him with her time, let alone her company.

***

She graduates with flying colours and although Uni doesn't interest her, she's not ready to tell me what she does want to do.  I firmly believe that she'll be moving out to pursue her adult life and I'm left hanging on tenterhooks waiting to find out when I'm going to lose her from my life.  My obsession with her was reaching fever pitch and I indulged and spoilt her outrageously in the lead up to the prom.  I went all out pampering her, hoping to live out my fantasies second hand.  Pretending I was preparing her for me not that cock stain she was still dating.

I even booked a spa day so she'd be perfectly polished.  A fully tailored dress that floated around her, making her look like an ethereal angel.  I even left her with an unlimited credit card at the upscale lingerie store so she'd could get whatever she wanted and beautiful from the skin out.

After all the preparation, it came down to the final minutes as we waited for Bruce to hopefully arrive on time and escort her to the prom.  God, I was consumed with jealousy.  I wanted the honour of her on my arm, I wanted to be the one holding her tight our bodies flush together as we danced. Gazing into each other's eyes, silently whispering promises for the later in the night.

As I sat twitching in torment I heard June's phone ring.  A call right before the dance, that didn't sound promising. There was a moment of silence after she answered and then there was a heartrending wail. Racing to her I find her a collapse sobbing mess on the floor, her phone clutched in her hand.  I gathered my broken princess in my arms as I tried to find out what had happened.

Stuttering and hiccupping through her tears she sobbed, "B..B...Bruuce duuumppped mmeee!  He... he… he saaiid he took <hiccup> Becka 'cause ssh.. sshhe..sshhhee was a sure thiiiiiiiinnnnngg an... an... and he wanted to get laaaaaaaaaiiiiiiiidd toniiiiiiight.”

I wanted to pound that inconsiderate shit stain into paste. How dare he break my sunshine like this?  I sat there holding her close, trying to get a grip on my protective anger when I had a sudden thought.

I could fix this.  I could make this a wonderful and magical night and at the same time, I could finally make my forbidden desires come true.  I quickly put a plan together in my mind and as June started to calm down I cupped her face, turned it to look up at me, thumbing tears from her eyes.

“Baby girl, do you trust me?” June gives me a watery smile and nods her head.

“Good girl” I praise her quietly, “I’m going to go and get organized.  I need you to finish calming down, tidy yourself up and wait for me here. I’ll be back in just a little bit, I love you.”

# Chapter 3

I pull the quickest date readiness in history as I mentally run through the list of things needed.  Carrying my shoes I pop back into the kitchen, call a gourmet dinner delivery from UberEats and pour a couple of glasses of wine. I put on some slow romantic music, move the lounge furniture to the edges and then dim the lights.  Finally I light some candles I found in the back of the pantry.

Once that's all done, I grab her wine and go and knock lightly on June's door.  She opens her door slowly and takes a step back in surprise as she sees me dressed in a tux.  I hold out the glass of wine and make an exaggerated bow after she takes it, "Good Evening young lady, is your older sister here?  I'm sorry I don't have a corsage, but I hope the wine will do. I'm here to escort her to the dance?"

The surprise on her face stays so long that I'm worried she won't join in, I'm relieved to see her flash a small smile and giggle, "Silly Daddy, you know it's me.  What are you doing?"

"Junie, I don't have a corsage for you, so I thought some wine would make up for that." I hand her the wine, she takes a sip as I place her arm in mine leading her towards the front of the house.  "This is your special, ultra-exclusive graduation dance.  Only the very best people are allowed to attend."

I slowly escort her through to the lounge room and let her see what I've put her together.  She stares in awe at the sort of, transformed lounge.  I bow to her, extending a hand "May I have the extreme honour of this dance my beautiful June?"  Putting her glass down on a close by shelf she takes my hand.  "I'd be honoured."

As the slow music plays through the house I waltz her around the room.  It feels so good with her in my arms, I slowly draw her closer so that in time our bodies start touching.  I catch her gaze with mine grin slyly, softly saying "You've grown so beautiful, I love you baby girl.  If you let me, you'll be mine forever."

I hear the UberEats driver drop off our special dinner, I gather it up and lay it out on the table.

"Daddy what did you do?  What's all this?"

"I told I would fix it all sweetling.  I don't want to let you out of my sight so we're having our special graduation dinner here.  Bring your wine over and sit down." I pull her chair out for her as she sits.

I use light conversation to divert June's mind from Bruce's awful behaviour and break the intensity of earlier.  Limiting her to only one glass of wine, I don't want her to be impaired for my plans for later.

She turns to me over dessert "I love you, Daddy.  You're the best there is, you've done such a great job fixing things and making this night real special.  I, I need to tell you something, please just let me speak."  I nod as she visibly sobers.

"I'm real proud that you didn't hassle me about what a douche canoe Bruce was.  I know you were thinking it, I could tell.  You treated me like a grown up and allowed me to make my own mistake.  I feel bad, but I'm so glad Bruce turned out to be such a wanker before the dance."

Standing I take her hand, slowly drawing her up and begin slow dancing with her.  Tucking her smaller frame in against me until our bodies are touching everywhere.  I've got her tucked in so tight that she can feel my erection pressing into her.  I'm concerned that I might be moving too fast but I can't stop.

I'm not sure what's happening at first.  Confused and convinced that it's just part of her dancing, but with little twitches and sighs she seems to be rubbing herself against my hard cock.  The longer I say nothing the more aggressive she seems to get.  I drop one of my hands to her delectably squeezable rear and start pushing her against myself in time with her twitches.  Flexing my abdomen and rubbing my throbbing cock against her.

Feeling her lithe body rubbing against me is almost more than I can bear.  I catch her eyes and lower my head to brush a butterfly kiss across her lips, waiting to see her reaction.  She sighs a moan and whispers "Oh Daddy.  Yes please."  I can see arousal blossom when her eyes dilate.  We move around the room in small steps, as we slowly tease each other to a fever pitch of arousal.

"It's a very naughty thing to behave this way baby girl," I pause to increase her worry and can see it working as her eyes grow anxious. "for anyone else."

I drop my head and take her mouth firmly, forcing her mouth open and stroking her tongue with mine.  Leading the way as I start teaching my girl how to kiss.  Amazingly she threads her fingers around my neck and through my hair, pulling my head to her's tightly as she tries to deepen the kiss.  I take this a full consent and unleash my desire on her.  Cupping her face in my hands I plunge my tongue into her mouth and devoured her.  We spend, what seems like hours, kissing and eating away at each other's mouths.

I glide my hands down her shoulders until I reach her breasts.  Running my hands around to cup them and take their weight, flicking my thumbnails over her nipples, eliciting a deep groan.  I thank the powers-that-be for strapless dresses and scoop her breasts out of the top, where their full C cup bounty is displayed and pushed up by the supports of her dress.  Keeping my touch firm but gentle I caress the firm flesh and continue to flick her diamond hard nipples.

As I lower my head preparing to see if these raspberry drops are as delicious I ask "Are you going to let anyone else see these?"

"No Daddy, they're only for you.  They've been yours since Mom left.  I didn't know how to tell you.  Wanting you like this is so wrong, that's why I tried to be with Bruce.  I couldn't stand to let him touch me because he wasn't you.  I've always wanted you to be my first and only.  Daddy, you're my everything, I want you to be my first tonight.  Fuck me and put your baby in me.  I want to bear all your children Daddy.  Their mother and your wife."

"I've felt the same forever baby girl.  I'm going to own every part of you, I'll fill you so full of cum that you'll forget what it's like not to be dripping my cum from somewhere.

I'll never let you go you're mine forever now." I growl as I drop and take a rock hard nipple in my mouth.  Sucking and pulling, grazing with my teeth before gently biting.  I suck hard leaving marks across her breasts as I half drag, half walk her to a lounge chair.

The chair is perfect. With good soft arms and enough back for her to lean against. I kneel at her feet and grab her ankles, scoot her to the edge of the chair and hook her knees over the arms of the chair as I run my hands up her legs, pushing her dress up to expose the playground hidden underneath.

Once she's fully revealed her I growl.  "Lace crotchless panties?  You are a very naughty girl.  Did you do this for me or for that stain?" I ask aggressively.

"No Daddy, Bruce would've got my granny panties.  He wasn't worth these.  I bought these for you, thinking that it was just a pipe dream." She tries to close her legs and hide her soaked pussy from view.

I grab her knees to stop their movement and use them to open her to my view again. "No sweet girl. Your legs stay open, now be a good girl for Daddy and hold your knees where I put them.  Good girl."  I use my hands to frame her soaked and shaved pussy peeking out of the panties.

"You're such a naughty little girl, thinking of your Dad that way.  Wanting to show me something I'm not supposed to see.  I'm so proud of you."

I rip the panties all the way open so there's nothing in my way.  Admiring her pretty petals open and pulsing, her clit peeking out and the copious dew drenching her thighs and leaking down her ass.  I lean in, catching her by surprise, and lick her from bottom to top using a flat broad single stroke. She squeals and tries to bring her hips closer to me for more.

"Oh God Daddy that feels so good, do it again, do it again?" she begs breathlessly.

Before I dive back in, I slip out my phone and start taking pictures of my baby girl's virgin pussy.

"Daddy what are you doing?  You shouldn't take photos of me like that. … Daddy!!"  She sits up and tries to close her legs in embarrassment.

After capturing her engorged and red clit I give her glistening pussy lips a light slap and say sharply "Enough Baby Girl!  You be a good girl for daddy and keep those knees where I told you to.  This, and I cup her entire cunt in my hand, is mine now."  I hold her pussy lips back to take some down the tunnel shots and continue "Sshh Baby Girl. I need to record this for later.  I want to be able to look at my beautiful virgin and untouched pussy when we're not together."

I lean back in and plunge my tongue deep in her honey pot, basking in her taste and smell.  Alternating short and quick with long and slow, I send her squirming around the chair until I growl at her to keep still and hold her down with one hand.  I use my tongue to strum her engorged clit using quick side to side motions to drive her closer and closer to release.  I start a finger circling and dipping into her dripping opening, working on keeping her on edge.  I want her riding the edge so hard that when I take her innocence she won't feel any pain.

As I push a single finger into such pristine territory she moans and thrusts her hips forward to try and fuck herself on my finger.  I can feel her barrier as she works herself on my finger.  "Oh God Daddy this is so much better than when I touch myself.  Don't stop, I want more.  I want you to be my first, to take me and breed me.  Fill me with your cum and give me your children."

It's all I can do not to come in my pants like some kind of untried boy.  I push a second finger into her stretching and preparing her for the intrusion of my 9 inch cock.

Advancing until I reach her barrier.  Pushing and stretching it in preparation.  I then set up a steady rhythm pumping rhythm, sneak in a 3$^{rd}$ finger and double my assault on her clit.  I need to drive her up and over her peak quickly now so she'll be nice and wet for my cock.  Shortly I can feel her channel start quivering and clamping down on my fingers as I give her the first of many orgasms.

It's all I can do not to plunge my rock hard cock deep into her quaking cunt.  As I ease her down from her orgasmic high I sit back to admire my work keeping my fingers stroking her channel & pussy softly.  Admiring the view I know I have to get more photos.  My baby girl is laying back blissed out and happy, perfect for getting some pictures of my good girls twitching and leaking cunt.  At the sound of the camera app, she starts to get worried again.

"Daddy why are you taking more pictures.  You already have some.  Why do you need more?"  She's clearly starting to shift over into whiney baby mode and I'm not going to allow that.  She's mine now and I own her cunt.

After capturing her engorged and red clit I give it a good tweak and a gentle but jarring slap.  "Quiet June.  Who does this pussy belong to?  Who owns this now?"  I cup her firmly and squeeze her lips and clit in my large hand as I dip 2 fingers back into her and press down on her clit.

"You Daddy, it belongs to you, just like all of me.  I'm sorry Daddy, I didn't mean to make you cross."

"Hold your pussy lips back so I can to take some good baby girl.  When things are quiet at work or I need to re-live this moment, I want to look at photos of my beautiful post cumming pussy and I stroke myself."

I continue slowly pumping I continue to take photos.  She makes a half-hearted attempt to object, but I do notice that she doesn't move her legs and gets wetter with the more photos I take.  Clearly, my girl has an exhibitionist streak.

Once I'm satisfied with the start of my photographic record I lean forward and start worshipping her magnificent breasts.  Using hands, tongue and teeth, aiming to drive her to the brink again before I drive myself deep into her. Making her my woman and filling her fertile, unploughed womb with my seed.  I pinch and nibble her diamond tip nipples while I slip 3 fingers back into her soaking pussy. Pushing up against her barrier, stretching and loosening it more.  Rubbing my fingers around her pussy and pumping them until I feel her start to twitch around me.  She's insane with need, begging me to let her cum for me, humping herself on my fingers trying to bring me deeper into herself.

Just when she's on the verge I place the tip of my cock at her entrance and hold her down so she can't fuck herself on my cock before I'm ready.

I growl "Look at me.  Give me your eyes so you know who you belong to."  Like the good girl, she is her eyes float open and pierce my soul.  Making it clear of her total surrender to my will.

I flick her clit and say "Who does this belong to?"

"You Daddy, it's yours forever."

"That's right!" I say as I slam past her barrier finally completing my claim.

She groans in a combination of pain & ecstasy as I push past her barrier throwing her into a mini orgasm.  Like the good girl, she is she doesn't take her eyes off mine.  I can clearly see her desire ramp up.  I set my thumb on her clit and lightly start drawing circles.  I want her to get used to the feeling of being full, making little thrusts to build her back up.

"From now on this juicy cunt is mine.  I decide what goes in it.  Only me." I tell her sternly, not that she's going to argue with me.  "Tell me" I order.

"It's your Daddy and you're the only one who can put anything in it.  Only you."  She moans.  I snap a few more photos, getting the red stain of her lost virginity clearly visible. Catching the view of her untried flesh stretching around mine.  This is going to be a fantastic photo album.

"Such a good girl." I praise her as I start moving again exerting all my control to keep the thrusts slow and long.  I don't know how long I'll be able to last.  I want to try and make this as mind blowing as possible, drive her to another shattering peak before I finish.

The feel of wet, tight, juicy, cunt gripping my cock, as if reluctant to let me leave its new 'forever' home, will break me soon.

"Oh God Daddy, fuck me, oh yes, harder, harder Daddy.  I need you to fuck me harder Daddy."  She screamed at me pulling her knees up higher so I can get deeper in her, closer to her fertile young womb.

"Daddy, I'm cumming, I'm going to cum Daddy."

"That's it baby girl, cum on my cock.  Cum all over your Daddies cock.  Show me how much you want my cum filling you and breeding our child.  Show me baby girl, show me how much you want my cum."  I grunt as I thread one hand down to strum her engorged clit.

"Daddy, I'm cumming, fill me with your seed Daddy, fill me full, make me a baby with your Daddy cum."  She screams as she twists and writhes beneath me cumming all over my cock.  I can feel her juices sliding down my balls to drip on the floor.  Feeling all this sets me off.  I'm pumping and shuddering, banging my cock against her cervix.  Trying to crawl as far into her unploughed womb as I can, as I shoot rope after rope of my strong seed into her.  Splashing across her fertile fields, drenching her insides.

Her pussy pulses and throbs around my shaft milking every last drop of baby batter from me.  We slowly come down from our mutual pleasure using soothing touches and gentle.  I make tiny little rocking movements to keep myself from going completely soft.

"We'll move away and get married baby girl.  That way we can be together without a problem.  You'll go to Uni and I'll find a new job and we'll build ourselves a great family.  I'll take care of it all little girl, I love you so much."

She looks at me with eyes full of love.  "I love you too Daddy.  I think I'll go and get an early childhood education degree. Then I can take care of our children better."  Coyly she looks at me "Why don't you grab that camera again and take some pictures of your cum pouring out of me?"

My cock jumps straight to full hardness again as I laugh. And then do exactly as she suggests before I plough her and fill her up all over again.

My family pulled ahead of me as I slowed down to appreciate the scenery.  They were just as eager to get to the camping spot as I was, knowing that the long hike was almost over.   I looked up towards the camping area hoping that it was empty.  I saw my son and step-daughter laughing as they raced each other through the trees trying to get to the shower block first.  A ritual they've been engaging in since we first started camping together 7 years ago when I married Maria.

Laughing at their antics Maria walked into my view and my breath caught.  She was as gorgeous as the day I married her.  Silky white blond hair, highlighting an amazing set of clear blue eyes.  D cup breasts flowing down to a thin waist and back out to a nice heinie that's perfect for cushioning me.  It's for this reason that I spend a considerable amount of time working out to keep myself in top shape.  She deserves it.

We were all tired after hiking all afternoon in the summer heat and then setting up camp for the night. Pete and I made a nice camp with the Aerodrome II Pro tent that we'd splurged on for our wedding anniversary.  Us 'men' collected wood and set up the fire pit for after dinner as my wife and stepdaughter prepared dinner.  It might've been freeze-dried and instant food, but we all knew it was going to taste like manna from heaven after the long, hard 3/4 day trek.  There's just something about food prepared out of door after a day of hard work.

We had just finished cleaning up and were relaxing in the relatively warm night air around the fire, feeling the ache in our muscles and trying to build the enthusiasm for smores. Suddenly, out of nowhere, the skies opened in a deluge that was so heavy it was like the lake was trying to move location.  We were forced to scramble getting everything into the large family-sized tent annex.  The hard rain only lasted for ten minutes or so, but it was enough to soak us all to the bone.  By the time we were in the annex and zipped-up against the elements, the rain had died down to a soft pitter-pat, the kind that says "I'm here to stay".  It was too late for us, though, we were all cold, wet, and miserable.

Maria laughed and said, "We need to get dry before we all catch our death of cold."

"WooHoo, pyjama party!" my son and daughter chimed-in with their agreement.

"Sure," I agreed. "Let's get a bedroom curtain set up so we can all get changed at once."

"Wait, honey!  We're sodden, we can't go in the sleep area like this, we'll flood it."

Maria directed us all to strip down, as far as we were comfortable, before stepping into the next part of the tent. Pete and I, men of the world, had no problems stripping to our boxers and briefs, Maria and Sophia played it much safer and kept their t-shirts on.  Sophia grabbed towels and passed them around whilst Maria and I partially zipped the curtain across one of the bedrooms.  Pete collected the woman's backpacks and put them in the enclosed bedroom area.  Darling Sophia shivered and mopped her long dripping hair to prevent a puddle on the floor near the door of the tent.  I couldn't help but notice how her nipples stuck out underneath her wet T-shirt and bra.  God, how she'd grown!  She was a real looker: long blonde hair like silk, nicely rounded grown-up breasts, a tiny waist, and a tight perky round butt that just ached to be plundered.

Once we had the curtain up, the girls went through to their side and started to change while Pete and I stayed on our side and did the same.

"Josh can we have the lantern?" my wife asked. "It's too

dark over here to see what we're doing."  Unzipping the curtain a little bit I slipped it through to her.

She set it down, but it must've been against the far wall because the girls' shadows fell across the curtain.  I didn't notice the shadow show at first, focused on drying off and getting into something warmer.  I did notice Pete quickly turning his back to me, which was strange.  He wasn't normally shy in front of me and I wasn't shy in front of him either, so I thought that it was weird for him to start now.  That's when I noticed the shadows on the curtain and saw the outline silhouette of my wife and daughter.  They were two naked beauties, perfectly outlined in the light.  It was like a soft-core porn flick of silhouettes just three feet from us.  As I stared, I felt myself starting to get hard and hurriedly turned my back just like Pete had.

So...that's why the poor kid got shy all of a sudden.  Well duh, I thought, I felt the same.

I tried to push it out of my mind and peeled my wet boxers off, putting on sweat pants and a T-shirt.  The dry clothing made me feel instantly warmer, but a chill was still deep in my bones and I know that the girls would feel it worse than me.

"Hey, hon?  Did you pack any booze?"  Usually, we would

take along some brandy or whiskey.  Liquid was heavy to haul in a pack, so we'd opt for the hard stuff...more punch for less weight.  It was great to have if we needed it for first aid, but usually, it served as a nightcap and a little touch of civilization on our camping trips.

"Yeah, smart thinking" my wife replied. "It's in the outside pockets of your pack."

"Oh, thanks! Make me tote it, huh?"

"The only way to travel pack mule. Heyah!"

While I was pissed at having been duped, I was grateful to my wife when I found four 200ml bottles of whiskey tucked amongst my socks and underwear.

"Wow. You weren't kidding around. How long did you think we'd be out?" I asked when I found it.

"Well, they predicted rain and I thought it'd be nice if we got caught in it.  Help warm us up a bit, you know, for medicinal reasons."

"Us? You mean the kids, too?"

My son, just pulling his T-shirt on over his head, looked at me with eyes as big as quarters.

"Well, I guess a few mouthfuls won't hurt," my wife said. "They're well over age."

"Sure, Dad," Sophia quickly added. "Pete and I are just as cold as you and Mom.  It's only fair."

I looked at my son and smiled.  "OK.  I guess we all deserve a sip or two.  It's been kind of a tough hike so far.  But you two be careful, no more than a couple of mouthfuls." I said looking at Pete. "I don't want to deal with drunk kids.  No getting sick and I *especially* don't want to have to deal with hangovers tomorrow."

"We won't dad," Sophia moaned from the other side of the curtain.

## Single Titles

Ruined Prom
Left at the Alter
Fixing Dad's Broken Box
Our Family Surrogate
Alone at the Park
Daddy's Wedding Present
Unexpected Dinner Date
Summer of Defiance
Children of the Farm

## Series

**Summer Camping**
- Part 1
- Part 2

**Alien Insect Bite**
- The Swarm
- Mating Preparation
- Mating Pool Expansion

- [Mating Plans](#)
- [Mating Dominance](#)
- [Mating Consequences](#)

## Family Medical Practice

- [My Brat](#)
- [Discovered](#)

# Bundles & Anthologies

[Summer Camping Bundle](#)
[Alien Insect Bite Bundle: Books 1-3](#)
[Alien Insect Bite Bundle: Books 4-6](#)
[Family Medical Practice: Duet Books 1 & 2](#)

Would you like Amazon to notify you when LL releases a hot new title?  Just click here to go the LL's <u>Amazon Author Page</u> and hit **Follow**.

<u>Facebook</u>
<u>Webpage</u>
Eden Books & PayHip – For those too Taboo for Amazon to publish.

PS – Check out my other works under other pen names.

<u>TB Fern</u> – for a taste of plants and insects.
<u>Preta Peth</u> – for a taste of demonic pleasure.

The author has been kicking around this world since 1972, but currently lives in Australia.  She has a wonderful husband, a daughter and son, all who have been incredibly supportive as she's been suffering with fibromyalgia since 2004.  She has worked hard to gain a quality of life and tried many different things to keep her mind occupied.

She finally decided to start writing as her mind is constantly inundated with stories and fantasies, but as she has family around the globe she writes her work under pen names.

Under the pen name LL Honi, she started writing in 2019. She writes fantasies about naughty little families.  Quick and dirty stories guaranteed to set your sheets on fire.

Welcome to the world of LL Honi, short and oh, oh so dirty. Join our fantasies as we enjoy blended families, first times and bareback breeding.

Additionally, leaving an honest review on Goodreads, Amazon or any other retail site would be appreciated. Reviews help cue readers into what they might like or dislike about a book and enhance book discovery.

I love to hear from my readers and make a point of answering every e-mail I receive. If you have any questions or comments, feel free to e-mail me at llhoni.author@gmail.com

Many thanks for reading.

Cover created using Canva
Formatting and editing all completed by author

person, please purchase an additional copy for each recipient. If you're reading this book and did not purchase, or it was not purchased for your enjoyment only, then please return to your favourite retailer and purchase your own copy.  Thank you for respecting the hard work of the author.

This book is written in Australian English there's every chance it may contain measurements, spelling, phrases, scenes & references peculiar to Australian Culture.  IE The legal drinking age in Australia is 18, and whilst all people in this book are over 18, the legal age for sexual conduct is 16.